DOROTHEA P9-DVU-559

JUST LIKE NEW

For my special English friends:
Ailsa, Angela, Clare, Jenny, Jill and Sandra
A M

For Mom and Dad—lest we forget
K R

Text copyright © 1995 by Ainslie Manson
Illustrations copyright © 1995 by Karen Reczuch
First published in the United States in 1996
All rights reserved. No part of this book may be reproduced, stored in a retrieval system or transmitted in any form or by any means, without the prior written permission of the publisher or, in the case of photocopying or other reprographic copying, a licence from CANCOPY (Canadian Reprography Collective), Toronto, Ontario.

Groundwood Books/Douglas & McIntyre Ltd.
585 Bloor Street West
Toronto, Ontario M6G 1K5

The publisher gratefully acknowledges the assistance of the Canada Council, the Ontario Arts Council and the Ontario Ministry of Culture, Tourism and Recreation.

Canadian Cataloguing in Publication Data

Manson, Ainslie
Just like new

ISBN 0-88899-228-9

I. Reczuch, Karen. II. Title.

PS8576.A57J8 1995   jC813'.54   C95-930168-2
PZ7.M35Re 1995

The illustrations are done in graphite pencil and watercolours
Design by Michael Solomon
Printed and bound in Hong Kong by Everbest Printing Co. Ltd.

JUST LIKE NEW

BY

AINSLIE MANSON

ILLUSTRATIONS BY

KAREN RECZUCH

A GROUNDWOOD BOOK

DOUGLAS & McINTYRE

TORONTO * VANCOUVER

DOROTHEA WALKER ELEMENTARY

Sally was snapped out of her daydream by the sudden silence. The shuffling, snorting and giggling had stopped and the whole Sunday school class was listening, really listening to their teacher, Miss Buxton.

"And because of the war," she said, "lots of children in England aren't going to have any Christmas presents at all this year."

Sally stared at her in disbelief. In Canada butter and eggs were hard to find because of the war, but shortages in England must be much worse if there were no presents!

"Next Sunday is White Gift Sunday," Miss Buxton went on. "I would like each of you to bring a gift, wrapped in white, for one of those children."

Sally decided she would use crisp white paper and a fluffy, flouncy bow. Her white gift would be extra specially magnificent.

"Your gift is not to be bought," Miss Buxton continued, "but it must be just like new. It should be something of your own, and it would be more meaningful if it was something you really loved."

Sally and her brother Jim walked home with Peggity Tompkins. Peggity was staying across the street with the Browns, but her real home was in England. She had come to Canada because of the bombs. It wasn't safe in her city.

Peggity and Jim were chatting but Sally wasn't listening. She swished through the falling leaves thinking about White Gift Sunday. Just like new, she thought. At least that meant she wouldn't have to give one of her books. Because of the war, books were scarce and she loved the few she had. She was glad they were worn and shabby.

"How come there are no presents in England for the children?" Sally asked Peggity.

"I expect the toy stores got bombed," said Peggity.

"No, that's not why," said Jim. "It's because they're using all the tin and wire and wood and paint that they usually use for toys to make wartime things instead—planes and tanks, guns and bullets."

"That's horrible!" said Sally.

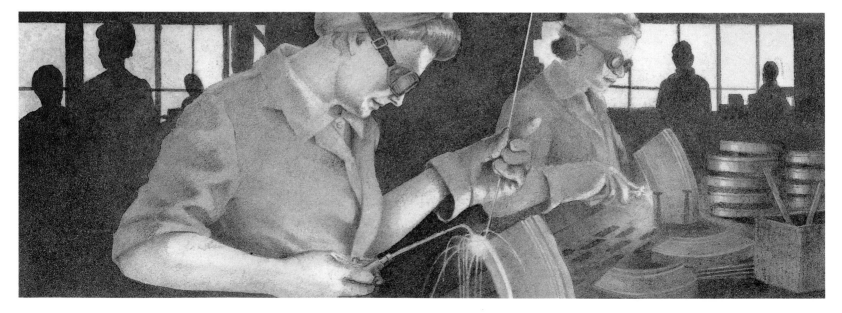

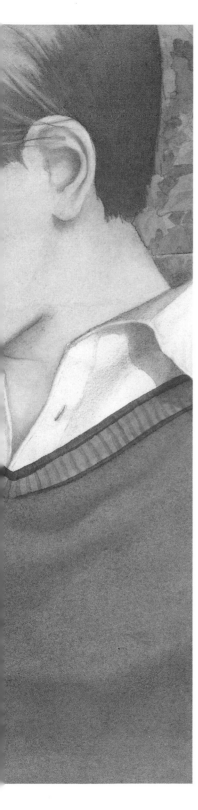

After Peggity turned in at the Browns' house, Sally and Jim walked on alone.

"What are you going to give?" Jim asked.

Sally shrugged. She hadn't decided.

"I'm going to give the book about flowers that Aunt Ethel gave me for Christmas last year," Jim announced proudly.

"But Miss Buxton said you're supposed to like the gift you send," said Sally. "In fact you're supposed to LOVE it."

Jim laughed and marched ahead. He liked to march like their dad had marched before he'd been wounded in the war. Left, right, left, right. But suddenly he did an about-turn and marched back. He blocked Sally's way and frowned down at her. "YOU," he said in his meanest big-brother voice, "YOU are the only one who knows I hate that book about flowers, right?"

"Right," said Sally.

"And you're the only one who will EVER know, right?"

"Right," said Sally again.

At dinner that night Sally and Jim told their parents about White Gift Sunday. Jim told them he was going to give Aunt Ethel's book about flowers. Sally squirmed when they praised him for his thoughtfulness. Jim gave her a kick under the table as a reminder.

"And what are you going to give, Sally?" Mum asked.

"I'm going to give one of my dolls," said Sally without hesitation. Mum looked quite surprised, but not as surprised as Sally felt. She had had no idea that she was about to say such a thing!

"Are you sure, dear?" Mum asked with a look of concern.

"Of course I'm sure," Sally said with a carefree toss of her head. "I'm too old for dolls anyway." But as she said it, she wondered how she could possibly give away Thelma or Susie or Ann Marie.

Dad got up from his chair and gave her a pat on the head. "A kind and thoughtful idea," he said. "And you do have three dolls, so you'll still have two when you send one away, won't you?"

Sally wasn't very good at arithmetic, but she had figured that out. She nodded, gave him a weak smile, then excused herself from the table.

"I have to give one of them away!" she whispered as she walked up the stairs. "Who will it be, who will it be? Thelma or Susie or Ann Marie?"

Thelma and Susie and Ann Marie just stared at her when she told them that one of them was about to go on a long journey.

Thelma was the oldest. Sally had had her for as long as she could remember. When Sally was very little, she cut Thelma's hair because she thought it would make her look pretty. It didn't. And now one eye stayed closed all the time, and two of her china fingers had chipped off. Miss Buxton would not approve of Thelma. Thelma was not just like new.

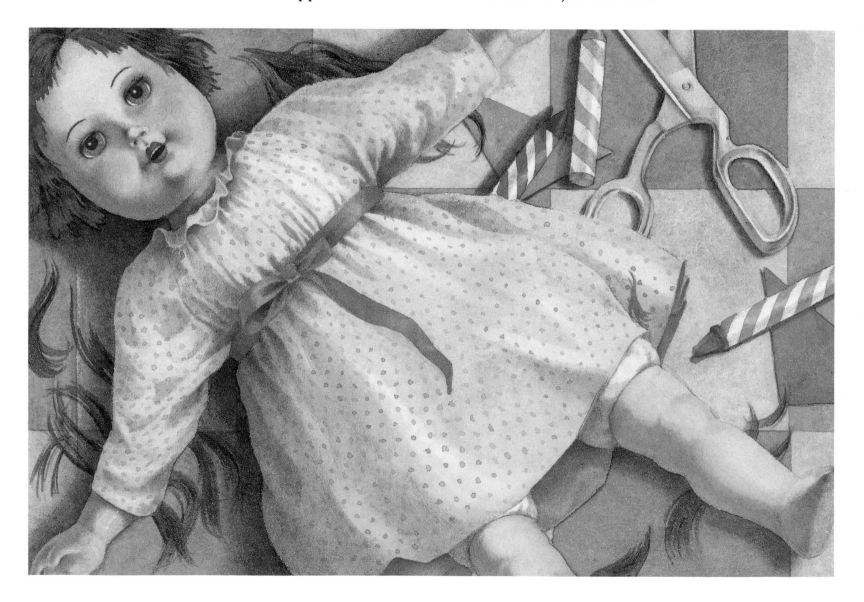

Susie was a rubber doll. She had a tiny hole in her pursed pink lips. When Sally gave her a drink Susie was supposed to wet through a tiny hole in her other end, but sometimes she wet through her left arm instead. The dog next door had made two rows of tooth holes in Susie's left arm when he had mistaken her for a bone. Just like the Red Cross nurse who had bandaged up her father's leg, Sally made a bandage to cover up the tooth holes, but Susie still wasn't in very good condition. Miss Buxton wouldn't approve of her, either.

That left Ann Marie. She was just like new. She had been a gift from Sally's godmother. Her eyes opened and closed and they were edged with long eyelashes. She had thick golden braids that Thelma envied, and she had smooth arms that Susie envied. She had come wearing a red plaid taffeta skirt, a dark-green velvet jacket with tiny shiny buttons, and a straw hat with flowers on its brim.

During the war Sally's dresses were passed on to her by cousins and friends, and when she grew they had extra bits added at the hemlines. Her mother explained that they had to share and "make do."

Sally had explained to Ann Marie about sharing and "making do." Now Susie wore Ann Marie's dark-green velvet jacket with the tiny shiny buttons. It covered her tooth-marked arm. Thelma wore Ann Marie's straw hat with the flowers on its brim. It covered her ugly bald head and made her almost pretty again.

"Just like new," Miss Buxton had said. So who would it be? Ann Marie, of course. Sally apologized to Thelma as she eased the elastic from under her chin and took back the straw hat. Then she apologized to Susie as she undid the tiny shiny buttons and removed the velvet jacket.

In all her finery Ann Marie looked perfect again. Sally tried not to think about her decision for the rest of the week.

The following Saturday afternoon Mum found a shoebox that Ann Marie would fit into. She also found white paper and a silky ribbon. Sally wondered a little about the ribbon, but when it was ironed, she had to agree that no one would ever guess it had once been a part of Aunt Ethel's petticoat.

Sally gently placed Ann Marie in the box and put on the lid. "I think she will go to Princess Elizabeth, don't you?" she asked her mum.

"No, I don't think that," said her mum, deftly folding the paper into sharp corners at either end of the box.

"Who, then?" Sally asked.

"I expect she'll go to a little girl just like you. A little girl who because of the war has a piece added to the hemline of her dress, just like you. A little girl who because of the war has darns in the elbows of her sweater, just like you. But a little girl, just like you, who doesn't have a doll because her country is being bombed."

Sally felt a lump in her throat as she placed her index finger on the ribbon for her mother.

Sally put the beautifully wrapped white gift on Ann Marie's empty chair. The room seemed extra quiet. Thelma stared at Sally with her one good eye. Susie stared at the white gift that was Ann Marie.

Sally lay on her bed and hid her face from them. She began to wonder about the girl "just like her" that her mother had told her about. Then she realized with horror that the girl wouldn't even know Ann Marie's name!

Sally found a piece of paper and a pencil. "Her name is Ann Marie," she wrote. "She belonged to me: Sally Nicholas, 4000 Melrose Avenue, Notre Dame de Grace, Montreal, Quebec, Canada, The World, The Universe. I liked her. Now she belongs to you. I hope you like her, too."

Then she carefully undid the ribbon, unfolded the paper and opened up the box. Ann Marie was asleep. Hoping she'd stay like that all the way to England, Sally slipped the note under her jacket. Folding the paper in the same places, she wrapped up the package again. It took ages, and she was just readjusting the bow that was somehow not as beautiful as it had been, when Jim appeared at her door.

"I was just thinking," he said. "I could give you my old bear, and you could send him instead."

Sally shook her head. He nodded. "I know," he said. "Old Bear isn't just like new."

Jim sat down beside her on the bed.

"How's she going to breathe?" he asked.

Sally looked at him in alarm.

"I know, let's stick straws in her nose," he suggested.

Before Sally could answer, Jim was off to the kitchen and back in a flash with two straws.

They carefully untied the ribbon again, unfolded the paper and opened up the box. Ann Marie slept on as Jim stuck one long straw in each of her nostrils. Then with a penknife he made two holes in the cover of the box so the straws could stick out. The hardest part was making holes in the wrapping paper as well, and then disguising them by tying the bow over them. The paper was now rumpled and smudged, and the bow lay limp except where the straws poked up.

It was snowing the next morning, and even though it was still October, the church looked like Christmas. They had brought the wooden baby Jesus out early so that everyone would remember that the white gifts were going to England as Christmas presents.

Sally liked walking down the aisle and placing her white gift beside the wooden baby Jesus...but she didn't like leaving it there.

Her brother Jim hated walking down the aisle and placing his white gift beside the wooden baby Jesus...but he was delighted to leave it there.

Sally thought about Ann Marie all that week.

On Monday her father explained that she probably wasn't even at the Montreal harbor yet.

On Tuesday her mother said Ann Marie would be on the boat, but she wouldn't have sailed off down the St. Lawrence yet.

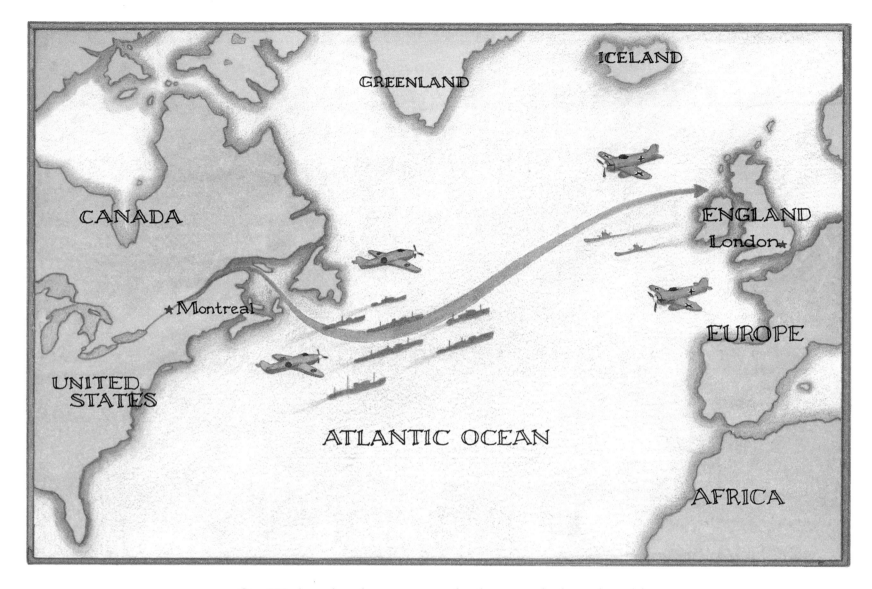

On Wednesday her parents both agreed that the ship
would have pulled anchor and sailed away. Sally wondered if
the straws were staying in Ann Marie's nostrils. She wondered if the box was lying down or standing on its end. If it
was lying down, Ann Marie's eyes would stay closed and she
would stay asleep. If it was standing up, her eyes would be
open and she'd have to stare at the inside of the dark card-
board box day after day, all the way to England.

"Is she there yet?" Sally asked on Sunday.

"She's somewhere on the high seas," Jim answered. He made high-wind sounds. He howled mournfully. He arched his right arm up and down, up and down, outlining the form of high waves. Sally felt seasick just watching him. Were the straws in Ann Marie's nostrils now? Were her eyes opening and shutting every time she went over one of those big waves? Sally wished they'd stuffed the box with something to keep her eyes closed.

She tried not to ask questions for the next few weeks.

Just before Christmas, though, Jim said, "Wouldn't it be awful if Ann Marie's ship got torpedoed?"

"Learn to think before you speak, Jim," Mrs. Nicholas said crossly, looking sideways at Sally.

When Sally began to cry, her father said in a voice of authority, "The ship arrived in England a good two weeks ago. You have nothing to worry about."

On Christmas day Sally thought about the little girl far, far away on the other side of the world opening the box and taking the straws out of Ann Marie's nostrils. She would sit her up, and Ann Marie would open her eyes and look around at her new country. Sally hoped bombs weren't falling on her town like on Peggity Tompkins' town.

Christmas was over and the new year began. Sally longed for news of Ann Marie.

Finally, on the first day of spring, the postman handed Sally an envelope with an English stamp on it. She opened it and carefully drew out a thin blue sheet of paper.

"Dear Sally," she read, "I thank you for your gift and I thank you for your note. I love Ann Marie. I especially love her green velvet jacket with the tiny shiny buttons, and her straw hat with the flowers on its brim. Ann Marie is my only doll. I will look after her carefully forever and ever. Love from Deborah. P.S. Let's be penpals."

"Yes, let's be penpals," Sally wrote back. "And give my love to Ann Marie!"

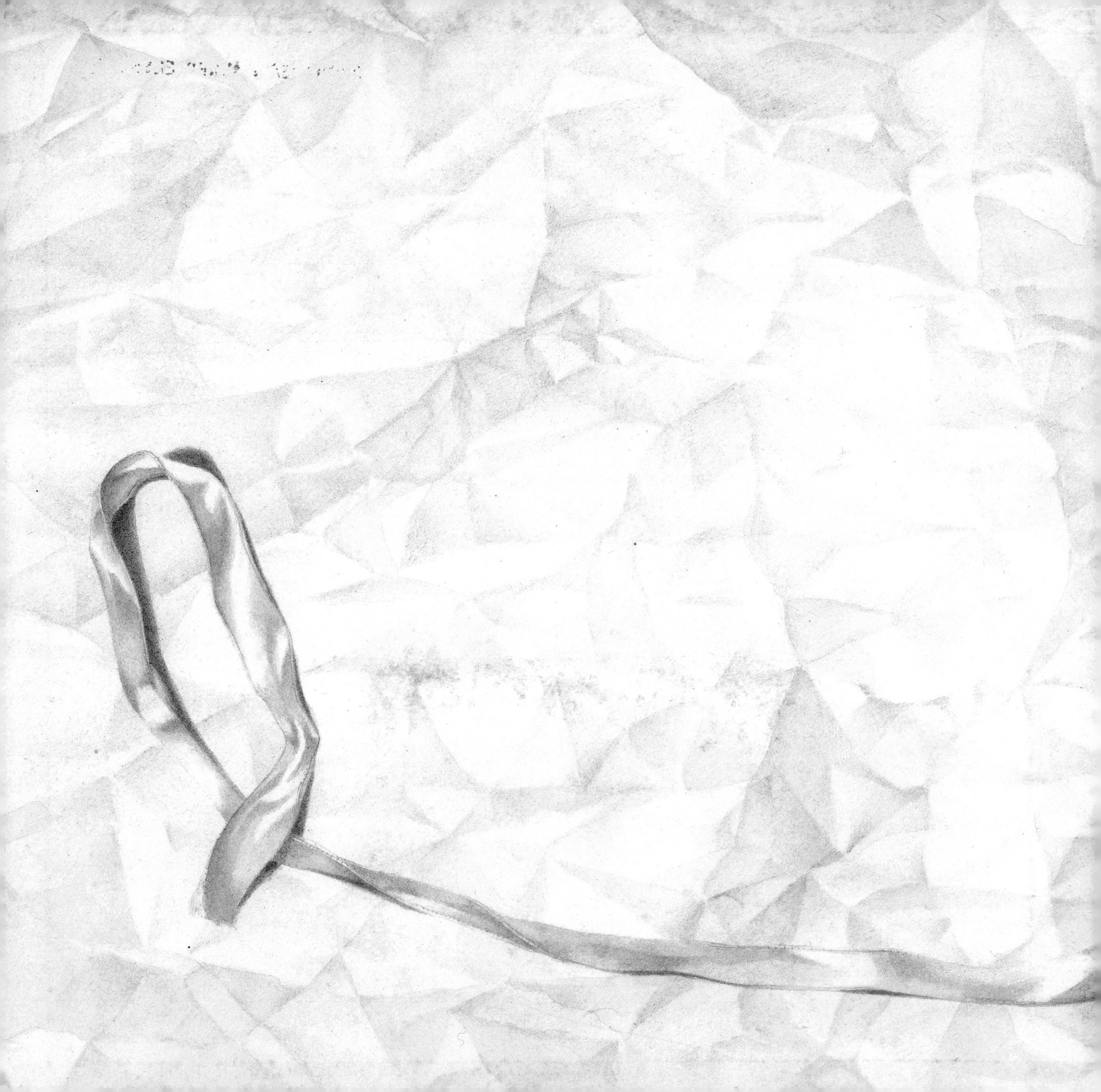